PAPER NIGHTS

design and graphic realization: Gilles Tibo

Annick Press Ltd.

Annick Press gratefully acknowledges the support of the Canada Council and
the Ontario Arts Council.

Canadian Cataloguing in Publication Data

Tibo, Gilles, 1951-
    Paper nights

ISBN 1-55037-225-4 (bound)   ISBN 1-55037-224-6 (pbk.)

I. Title.

PS8589.I26P3   1992   jC843′.54   C91-095750-9
PZ7.T5Pa   1992

The art in this book was rendered in ink with airbrush. The text has been set
in Baskerville bold by Attic Typesetting.

Distributed in Canada and the USA by:
Firefly Books Ltd.
250 Sparks Avenue
Willowdale, Ontario   M2H 2S4

∞ Printed on acid-free paper.
Printed and bound in Canada by
D.W. Friesen and Sons Ltd., Altona, Manitoba

GILLES
TIBO

PAPER NIGHTS

Story by Pierre Filion from an idea by Gilles Tibo

ANNICK PRESS
TORONTO, CANADA

On Pikolo's birthday his mother gave him some beautiful paper. That night he cut out his favourite animals to keep him company.

Pikolo and his mother decorated his room with the different cut-outs he had made. They taped them to the walls and strung them from the ceiling over his bed, so they floated and turned slowly around him. Pikolo felt as if he was in the middle of a jungle; he could hear the animals calling to each other from far away.

Pikolo would often spend his bedtime talking to them and telling stories. Then he would take out his scissors and cut out more new friends. He loved the crisp *snip snip* sound the scissors made as they cut through the paper.

One night he had already cut out a six-legged cat, a turtle with oars and was working on a whale with wings. He was busily imagining the land they lived in and how the whale was going to rescue the cat, and soon he was so excited he forgot to sleep.

He took out his most beautiful paper and started to cut out a little man. He topped him off with a large hat of flecked shiny paper that made Pikolo feel as if he was in the middle of the night sky with stars all around him. As he finished cutting, the little man opened his eyes.

"Hello, Pikolo! My name is Max. But hurry, we must go! They're waiting for us! Come with me."

"Where are you going? Why are you going into my closet? It's dark in there!"

But the little man was already on the other side of the door.

He looked so eager to leave that Pikolo quickly bundled up his favourite toys and hurried towards the closet.
"You don't need to bring those! There will be lots to play with."
Then Max disappeared into the deepest, blackest part of the closet.

Pikolo was afraid of the dark because he was frightened of what the dark might be hiding. But he knew the little man was just ahead, so he followed Max through the darkness for a very long time. Suddenly, hc saw a blue light in the distance. From it came a strange, sweet music that sounded like the voices of children.

They arrived in a place full of children who danced around him and clapped their hands.
"Hello!" they sang. "Come on! Come and see our secret."

They took his hand and before the time it takes to turn a page, they were in a world that made him stare and stare.

It was a land made of paper! Beyond the purple houses he saw children
splashing in paper seas and playing with whales the colour of pumpkins.
When he looked up in the sky, he saw more children flying paper airplanes
in and out of candy-coloured stars. There were paper people and wild
animals, boats and bicycles and swings that took you up past the moon.

Max smiled at Pikolo. "Didn't you know that while parents sleep, all children's closets become tunnels to this world? But remember, everyone must return before your parents wake up. Go play, Pikolo, you have until sunrise to play with your new friends."

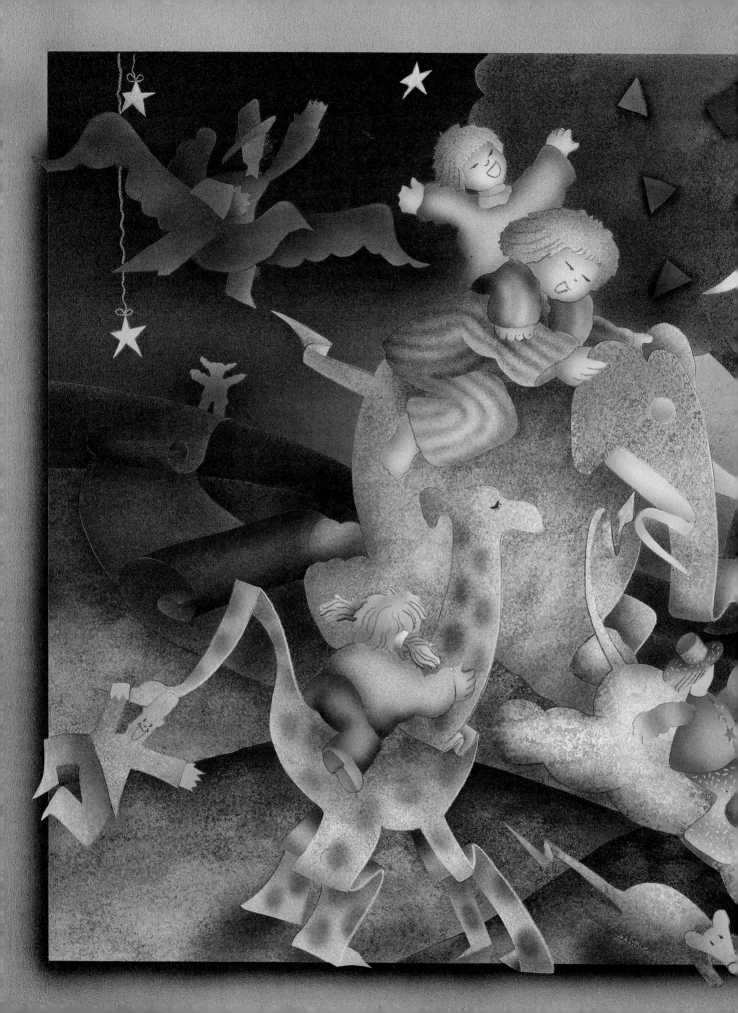

When the wild animals went to sleep, Pikolo still wasn't tired. He wanted to go back to the sea-green boat he'd found. He would sail it far from shore and watch fish the colour of stars fly out of the sea and dance around him.

Suddenly his new friends started to say goodbye.
"Don't leave!" Pikolo said looking around him. "Max, I don't want to go."
Max looked at him. "You must go, Pikolo. Everyone must go."

But Pikolo wasn't listening. He started to run to the beach to the boat that was the colour of the sea.

He hardly heard Max shouting, "Pikolo, stop! It's almost dawn."
Max called to his paper friends to help bring Pikolo back.

"Pikolo! Pikolo!" Max shook his head as they caught up to him. "We must hurry now, before the tunnels to the closets disappear."
One of the paper men put Pikolo on his shoulders. They quickly ran down

one tunnel which ended suddenly. But Pikolo thought he recognized a light in the distance.
"Max, look. Maybe that's the light from my bedroom."

They followed it to its end, but when they opened the door to the bedroom, Pikolo was surprised to see his friends Natalie and Roxanne, who lived two streets over, asleep in their beds.

"Do all the tunnels connect to each other?" asked Pikolo as they looked
into another bedroom that wasn't his.
"Yes, yes." Max was already racing back down the tunnels. "But we must
hurry, we have only a couple of minutes."

At the last second, Pikolo peeked into his own bedroom. "Max. We're here!
I found it!" Then he yawned a big sleepy yawn. Pikolo told Max it was
time to go to sleep and said goodnight to his toys, his paper animals, and his
bed.

Pikolo snuggled under his comforter. He closed his eyes and slowly, very slowly, he felt himself rocked to sleep by a swing suspended from the moon. Soon he was dreaming that he was swooping and diving on paper airplanes in and out of candy-coloured stars. Far off in the distance he could hear the wild animals calling.